The Moonlight Thrills Series: The Complete Collection

The Moonlight Thrills Series

Genevieve Leanne Dominguez

Published by Genevieve Leanne Dominguez, 2023.

Also by Genevieve Leanne Dominguez

The Moonlight Thrills Series
Moonlight Thrills
Starlight Adventure
Evening Dangers
Midnight Perils
The Moonlight Thrills Series: The Complete Collection

Standalone
When I Dream of You
Phoenix: A Small Poetry Collection

Watch for more at https://genevieveleanne.wixsite.com/mysite.

To my mom, Elsa. Thank you for believing in this series.

Moonlight Thrills

1

Chapter 1

The routine is simple. I open the store at noon. Jared comes in an hour later. He picks out a book and sits in the armchair near the window. I offer him something to eat or drink during my lunch hour, but he declines. Katie comes by in the evening and talks about her day. When Jared leaves, she dissects every gesture he made (which isn't a lot), insisting he's attracted to me.

"I've heard wolves can get attached quickly. It's sweet," she says with a faraway look. I can't help but smile every time she does that. Katie loves romance and firmly believes in interspecies relationships.

I believe in it too along with equality for all species – humans, wolves, vamps, fairies, wizards, etc. But, for whatever reason, wolves have been deemed inferior by everyone. Katie and I have theorized it's because everyone's secretly afraid of what they represent: animal passion.

"If he was interested, wouldn't he have talked to me by now? Maybe he just likes to read," I say as I flip over the sign on the door so that it reads "Closed". Katie shakes her head and steals my last cookie from my single serve pack.

"Want to bet on it?" she asks in between bites with a twinkle in her eye. If I say no, she'll know I'm attracted to him and will eventually convince me to flirt, which I'm terrible at.

"Fine, but I doubt he remembers my name," I say, heading over to a shelf where a book has been stuffed in the wrong place. Katie squeals and squirms excitedly before assuming a conspiratorial expression.

"Ask him something. If he ends the conversation, I'll stop talking about him. If he doesn't, I'll get the satisfaction of knowing I'm always right."

I make a face to which she smiles sweetly. She knows I don't like making the first move.

• • • •

When I'm snuggled under the covers in my bed, I go back to the beginning. Jared showed up at my bookstore two months ago. I recognized he was a wolf by his tattoo. By law, every species is required to get one to distinguish what we are.

He was hesitant and fidgety. His hands were shoved in his pockets and he glanced around, as if he was planning on making a run for it. I welcomed him as much as I could, hoping that I wasn't coming across as fake or overbearing. After browsing for a few minutes, he left. I expected him to never show up again. Yet, he did the next day. And the day after.

I glance at the tattoo on my forearm. The block letter "H" is enclosed in an intricate sun. The fine details, such as the curved lines and pointed tips, make me wonder... Has Jared ever experienced outright hatred because of who he is? He must know I'm not racist, otherwise he wouldn't have come back. Even if Katie's wrong and he doesn't see me in that way, I'd still like to be his friend.

I turn off the lamp on my nightstand and roll over to gaze at the full moon. The suburb I live in is only 20 minutes away from the city, but a forest is near its southern border. My bedroom window faces it, and it provides relaxation whenever I can't sleep.

What is it like to run between the fir and pine trees? To kick back the undergrowth, unaware of where you're going. The moonlight filters through the trees, creating prickly shadows of drooping branches and broken logs. You can sense the danger that lies ahead, but you're not afraid because you can rip apart anything that comes your way with your strong jaws and sharp teeth. The muscles in your legs ripple, urging you to run faster, as the wind caresses your fur.

This is what I want to ask Jared: What is it like to unleash your natural-born freedom?

I'd never admit it to Katie, but I took extra time to pick out my outfit today. I roll up the sleeves of my black sweater, feeling exposed in my jean shorts. My pinky toe rubs against the inside of my ankle boots as I straighten the shelves for the third time. The discomfort distracts me from the looming silence.

I head back to the front and work on the spreadsheet for inventory. It doesn't take long because I keep up with it on a daily basis, so I opt for mindless gazing.

My bookstore isn't really my bookstore. I manage it for the owner who owns multiple stores across the U.S. She works remotely because she likes to travel. I've met with her a few times in person. She's extravagant with a penchant for dark red lipstick and metallic blue eyeshadow, but she's nice and easygoing. As long as sales are good, she lets me do whatever I want with the store.

Glittery tea lights are on every table. String lights frame the large window. Faux greenery drapes over the top of the bookshelves. Pumpkin spice fills the air. I inhale deeply and concentrate on diminishing the fluttering in my stomach.

When the bell above the door dings, I don't need to open my eyes to know it's him. A bright, wide smile springs across my face. I tone it down immediately as he disappears among the shelves. I only caught a glimpse, but it looked like he was concerned. Alert.

I start to mentally list the excuses I'm going to tell Katie tonight to explain why I didn't talk to him. She'll tease me for chickening out, but I don't care. I can always talk to him tomorrow.

The day goes by slowly. Customers trickle in and out. The sky darkens at three. Thunder rumbles loudly at four. Jared is rigid the entire time. A lock of dark hair falls over his furrowed brows as he shrugs off his jacket. The only reason I know he's actually reading is because his eyes scan the page at a consistent speed. If he senses me looking, he doesn't react to it.

When it's lunchtime, I debate on whether I should offer him something. I decide to do it, but he sticks to the routine and declines. I count the number of leaves that fall from a tree to the sidewalk as I eat. Two crimson, three gold, one orange.

As I throw away my paper bag, Jared lays the book on his lap and closes his eyes. His forearm is turned to where I can see his tattoo. "WW" is set within a crescent moon. It's then I realize that, out of all the magical species, humans and werewolves complement each other the most. We are the sun and they are the moon. Opposites in unity.

A sheet of rain comes down hard outside. The *pitter-patter* is harsh against the roof. I text Katie, telling her to stay safe when she comes over. She works in the city and traffic gets crazy during bad weather.

I head to the back of the store to make sure the emergency exit is locked. Traffic isn't the only thing that gets crazy when it rains.

"Danielle?" Jared says. I spin around, banging my arm against the door handle. He winces and raises his hands slightly, silently apologizing for startling me.

"No, it's okay. I'm fine," I say. He relaxes a bit but remains silent.

"I didn't think you remembered my name," I say, smiling to lighten the mood. He smiles a small smile.

"I just wanted to say thanks for letting me stay throughout the day these past months."

"Of course. It's nice having someone here all the time, especially when it's a slow day," I say. He gestures to the shelves.

"I plan on buying every book I've read. I've been in between jobs, but I finally got hired today," he says. Why didn't I think about that before? I would've offered him a job. Instead, I assumed everything else but that possibility.

"It's no problem, really. Where are you going to work?" I ask. He leans against the wall and crosses his arms. The muscles in his biceps flex slightly. The black V-neck he's wearing looks so soft. My cheeks heat up when I start to imagine what his chest looks like. I snap my attention to his face.

"It's in the city. I'm going to be a content writer for a magazine."

"That's amazing!" I exclaim. He looks down as he smiles. The same lock of hair that fell into his eyes earlier falls again. His hair is a beautiful dark brown shade. It looks naturally windswept, and the ends barely grace the nape of his neck. When he looks at me, his dark eyes flash dark gold. A wolf's eye color. I gasp at the sight.

Jared mistakes my reaction for fear because he clears his throat and takes a step back. I dash forward, reaching out to touch his arm.

"No, I'm not afraid. I've just never seen a wolf change before. It's beautiful."

I look up at him, hoping to see it again. His eyes search my face then he glances at where I'm still touching him. I draw my hand back as my stomach flips over. Was that flirting? I don't want him to think I'm throwing myself at him.

He slowly backs me up against the door, extending his arms until he's boxed me in. I can't hold in my delighted, shaky breaths. He looks feral. Hungry.

"Danielle," he breathes.

Laughter coming from the front of the store breaks the tension. My legs are wobbly as I head to the front. Jared follows me. My heart beats fiercely as I replay what happened. If nobody had come in, what would he have done? Fantasies of him ravaging me flash through my mind. I stumble as I round the corner. Jared catches me, his hands firm on my waist and arm.

The laughter stops. A group of people throw suspicious looks at Jared. From the way he caught me, they must've seen his tattoo. The oldest woman in the group looks at my forearm. After she confirms I'm human, she smiles warmly.

"Are you okay, dear?" she asks. Jared lets go of me, but I grab his hand and our fingers intertwine.

"Yes, I am. Can I help you with anything?" I ask. She doesn't hide her sneer.

"No, thank you. In fact, I believe we have the wrong store. I didn't realize your lovely establishment was pet-friendly."

She lifts her head high and nods to the rest of the group. When they exit, Jared exhales.

"Does that happen a lot?" I ask.

"Every day," he replies.

"Why? What is it about wolves? You're no different from the other magical species," I say. He looks at me with an amused expression.

"I thought you and Katie figured that out already."

It takes me a few moments to realize what he's saying.

"How long have you been listening in on our conversations?" I ask. His smile lights up his face. He lets go of my hand to encircle my waist and pulls me closer.

"Long enough to know that you're beautiful. In every way."

I rise on my tiptoes and run my fingers through the ends of his hair. A low growl escapes from him. I pull back quickly, pushing down my embarrassed giggle. Katie's going to be so proud.

"Can I walk you home tonight?" he asks. His voice is husky. It suddenly occurs to me how tiny I am in comparison to him. Granted, I've always been naturally slim, and Jared's not bulky or overly muscular, but to be with him in that way...

I nod because I can't speak. Jared doesn't seem like a player. I don't feel that he would pressure me for sex. As much as I want it, I'm definitely not initiating it because I don't want him to think I do this with every man I find attractive.

The rest of the day passes by quickly. No more customers come in. The rain doesn't slow down. After the sun sets, Jared becomes rigid again. He glances around every few minutes and cranes his neck to stare out the corner window. His hands ball up into fists and his breathing grows heavy.

"Is everything okay?" I ask. He shakes his head and heads for the door.

"Can you call Katie and tell her not to come over tonight? I need to get you home now."

He flips over the "Open" sign and shuts off the lights. I fumble for my phone as goosebumps rise on my arms. I've never seen Jared like this. While the line's ringing, I notice movement out of the window.

The rain makes it difficult to see clearly, but I can make out two figures. One is average height and curvy and the other is large and hovering. I move closer to get a better look. Jared tells me to step away from the window just as the large figure punches Katie. She crashes to the ground. My eardrums pound and the phone falls out of my hand.

I rush out of the store, yelling her name, but she's unconscious. Her body is draped over the man's shoulder, hands limp and arms swinging.

He whirls around with an excited gleam in his silver eyes. His teeth are bared. They elongate and become pointed. He snaps his jaw. Jared grabs me from behind, dragging me backwards. I scream at him to help Katie, but he doesn't listen.

I'm helpless as my best friend is taken away.

"Why didn't you help her?" I shout once we're back in the store. His hair is matted to his forehead and his eyes are frantic. His shirt sticks to his skin, revealing the strong outline of his upper chest and abs. He's blocking the exit, so I push him aside.

Jared yanks me back and pins me against his chest. I kick and claw at him, even though I know there's no point.

"He was after you! He wants you, not her," he yells.

"All the more reason to save her!"

I gasp for air as the thought of Katie never being found enters my mind. Jared's grip loosens when I burst into tears. It happened so fast. I didn't think to call the police. Even if I called them now, there's no way of knowing where he took her. Unless he has priors and is in their system.

I scramble to get my phone, but Jared is faster. He's in front of me, holding out his hands.

"The police aren't going to help. He knows some of them," he says. That's when I finally stop. My sweater feels like a clumpy, wet blanket. My legs and feet are freezing. I push my hair out of my face and stare him down.

"How do you know that?" I ask.

"Because I used to be in his pack," Jared says. His expression is solemn. He drops his hands but doesn't move. Thunder claps hard. Lightning illuminates the darkness for a moment. His shadow reaches to the ceiling.

"Why did you leave?" I ask.

"He got into some bad things, shady businesses. He wanted the rest of us to be a part of it, but I didn't want that life."

"Why is he after me?"

"He swore he wouldn't let me live in peace. He feels like I betrayed our kind," Jared says. He crosses his arms and looks away.

"I thought I was being careful, but he tracked me down. I'm guessing he's been watching me long enough to know how I feel about you. I sensed him today, but I didn't want to believe it," he adds quietly.

"Do you have any idea where he's taking Katie?" I ask. Jared nods and bends down to retrieve my phone.

"It might be difficult to track him if he's not where I think he is. He chose tonight because he knew it was going to rain. He's luring you and me because he wants the chase."

He holds out my phone, but I crash into him instead, wrapping my arms tight around his waist. His damp shirt cools my cheek. I know I'm using his feelings for me to coerce him into helping, but it's for Katie. I need to do everything I can to rescue her.

"Please help her," I whisper, gripping his shirt. After a few seconds, he sighs and kisses my hair.

"You can't leave my sight. We stick together, no matter what," he says. I nod and murmur my gratitude. Jared pushes back slowly and tells me to turn around.

The sound of him unzippering his jeans is intense in the chilled air. I shift my weight to try to get some warmth in my body. I hear toenails clicking on the linoleum and loud sniffles a few seconds later.

Fur brushes against my thigh. Jared's wolf form is breathtaking. He's a bit larger than an actual wolf, as if his human height wants to take over. His features are refined and regal, and his fur color is the same as his hair. He taps my arm with his nose and licks me. I pet his head and scratch behind his ears. His dark golden eyes stare at me adoringly. He heads to where his clothes are and nudges the pile.

"Right. On it," I say, heading over to pick them up.

Next, he lies on his stomach and spreads his body wide. He dips his head low then brings it back up, motioning me to do something.

"Do you want me to climb onto your back?" I ask. He repeats the same motion. Carefully, I adjust myself and wrap my arms around his neck. Once we're outside, he crouches into a running stance. I stroke his fur and relax into him.

"Let's go," I say.

Chapter 4

The city is alive tonight. Cars race down the streets with the windows down and rock music blasting. Skyscrapers are lit from top to bottom. Neon signs advertise drinks, dancing, food, and more. Most people carefully avoid eye contact with me and dramatically sidestep Jared.

He takes us to an alley where the light is soft. I slide off him and lay his clothes on the ground before turning around to give him privacy. While he's changing, I rub off any streaks of mascara that might still be on my face and try to make my hair look presentable. Jared touches my shoulder when it's okay to turn around.

"David would come here every night after he got off work. He became good friends with the owner. He's inside right now," he says, pointing to the building on our right. The back door is labeled "Complimentz – Employee Only Entrance".

Complimentz was in the news a few weeks ago. It's a franchise tailored to magical species, specifically those who like humans. Humans are the only species who can be employed, and, essentially, it's a restaurant with the option to buy a compliment from a human. You can buy as many as you like, but each one costs $200.

Katie wanted to work there, but I discouraged her. Although I admired their public stance against racism toward magical species, it always seemed like one step above prostitution. One of their locations was recently involved in laundering money. A secret room was exposed where more than compliments were taking place between people.

Jared slides his hand in mine and grips it. When we're at the end of the alley, he hesitates. I squeeze his hand for reassurance.

"We can do this," I say.

When we enter, it's as if we stepped into a different world. Instead of walls, there are mirrors and the ground is made of glittery glass. Almost all the workers are dressed provocatively. The women wear miniskirts and the men are shirtless. Some are bussing or waiting on tables. Others are sitting at tables or booths designed to seat only two, talking in hushed voices to the person across from them. I can tell which ones are human because their tattoos are outlined in metallic marker.

The hostess asks us if we would like a table, but Jared tells her we're headed for the bar. She smiles and gestures us forward. His palm is sweaty, but I hold on tight. I know he's afraid for me. He said David wanted the chase, which means he has something planned. I push away my anxiety and focus on finding Katie.

David's laughing with the bartender. Used slices of lime and empty shot glasses are on the counter. A large plate of ribs sits in front of him with half of them already eaten to the bone. He turns around with a rib in hand and a triumphant expression on his face.

"Did you really think I wouldn't find you?" he asks.

"Took you much longer than I expected," Jared replies. David chuckles and glances at me up and down.

"She smells good. How long have you been mated?"

Jared's shoulders bristle. David bursts out laughing and sets the rib down. He wipes his hands and beard with a dirty napkin.

"Leave it to you to mate with someone you haven't even taken out on a proper date yet. This is why you'll never win, brother. I know you."

"I'm not your brother," Jared growls. David stands and claps his hand hard on Jared's shoulder. The sound of it makes me jump. He towers over Jared, which makes me feel like a bug he could flick and send flying across the room. I remember his wolf's teeth. The image of Katie's throat being ripped to shreds flashes in my mind.

"Nobody accepts us. We have to look out for each other. As a peace offering, I'll let you keep Danielle. No one in our pack will be able to lie with her."

Jared bares his teeth and pushes me behind him. David grins, as if he's enjoying that he's riling Jared up.

"Where's the girl you took?" Jared asks.

He shrugs.

"I have my own business to settle with her. Imagine my delight when I found out we're all connected."

He steps closer and jabs his finger in Jared's chest.

"Imagine the pain when you realize you've led your mate to her death," he says.

The ground rumbles slightly, causing the shot glasses to wobble and clink together. I grab Jared's arm. Raised voices come from behind us. Someone asks if it was an earthquake.

David backs away from us, narrowing his eyes at Jared. "If you don't die from the explosion, I'll make sure to finish the job."

He's gone in an instant. Chunks of glass spray upward from the ground. The mirrors crack and shatter simultaneously. Screams and pounding footsteps ensue. Jared yanks me to the right as a chunk of the ceiling crashes down where I was standing. The smell of smoking debris fills my nose. My nails dig into Jared's arm.

He scoops me up and heads to the back entrance. When we're outside, he doesn't stop. He breaks into a run and takes us far down the business strip. He slows down after he rounds the corner and sets me down.

"Are you okay?" he asks. His voice is gruff as he inspects me.

"I'm fine. What about you?" I ask. He shakes his head and pushes his hair out of his face.

"That was too close. Had I been off one second, you would've died. I never suspected..."

He trails off and closes his eyes, his chest heaving deeply. He bends over and rests his palms on his knees. What David said about Jared mating with me crosses my mind. How is that possible if we haven't even kissed?

I softly rub his back. "But you weren't too late. You saved me," I say.

As Jared's breathing slows down, I spot David up ahead. Katie's with him. Her eye is swollen and there are bruises on her arm.

"Danielle!" she screams. Jared jerks upright. David turns around and throws her over his shoulder. She shrieks and shouts for me again. Everyone on the sidewalk moves out of the way. No one attempts to call for help.

"You'll only be able to save one of them," David shouts. His laughter becomes distorted and is drowned out by the sound of traffic when he begins to run.

David disappeared while we were still in the city, but Jared tracked him to the forest. The canopy of branches overhead scatters the moonlight. Rain drips from the leaves and onto the hardpacked dirt. The soothing aroma of rain and pine doesn't help calm the trembling in my body. We walk slowly, stopping every few seconds so Jared can keep David's scent.

David said he had business to settle with Katie. How did they know each other? She would've mentioned if she had dated him. I rack my brain for anything she may have said in passing that could tie back to him.

A couple of branches snap to my right. I gasp and lean into Jared. A gnarled log with several holes in its bark is propped against a wide tree trunk. A squirrel scurries out of one of the holes.

"Put your back against a tree," Jared whispers. We break from the path. Fallen leaves rustle from my hurried steps. He presses his back against me, whipping his head from left to right and sniffing hard. Slowly, he inches forward and peels off his shirt.

David tackles him from the side. I scream as he pins Jared down. He snarls and raises his hand high. His fingers are curved and his claws are positioned to cut deep. I spot a thick branch nearby and grab it.

David grunts when I hit him on the head and swings his fist back. I skid across the forest floor and bump into the base of a trunk. Jared's shouts shift into growls. The back of my head burns. Warm liquid slides down the side of my head and into my ear. I struggle to regain control of my body.

Muffled screams distract me from my pain. I squint in the darkness, trying to determine where they're coming from.

"Katie?" I shout.

Jared and David are in wolf form, circling each other. When David and I make eye contact, he crouches low and jumps over Jared. My scream echoes across the forest. Somehow, I'm up and running fast.

"Danielle, stop!" Jared says.

I stop near a large, deep hole. A huge tree to my left has been cut down. Half of the trunk lies over the hole. A thick rope is tied around it with Katie dangling by her wrists over long wooden spikes.

Something hard makes contact with my spine. Pain shoots through the center of my back. I wheeze as all the air is knocked out of me. David turns me over so that my head is over the hole. He squeezes my throat and thrusts his knee in my stomach. My vision blackens as I struggle to pry his hand off.

His weight is lifted off me in seconds. I cough for air and curl up to ease the aching in my stomach.

"All of this to hurt me? Even the explosion? Those were innocent people!" Jared says.

"The explosion wasn't for you, but it would've been a perk if you had died," David replies.

From my peripheral vision, I see them facing off. They're naked and covered in sweat, blood, and dirt.

"What are you doing? What is all this?" Jared asks. David bends down and begins morphing into a wolf.

"Right now, I'm killing your mate, " he says. Jared barrels into him, switching into a wolf as well. I move to the side as their fighting brings them closer to the hole. The thought of Jared being punctured by a spike helps me think clearly.

I stand and veer to the left. David snaps at Jared and moves to keep me in his sight. Jared's blocking him as best he can, but I see the rage pulsing in David's eyes. His fur bristles on his back as he swipes at Jared.

"Move," I whisper to Jared. His ears shoot straight up, pausing for a second. That's exactly what David – and I – need.

He jumps high in the air, limbs extended and jaw wide open. At the last second, I fall flat on my back and kick hard. The heels of my boots dig deep into his stomach. The force of it causes him to fly backward into the hole. He whines and scrambles to get back on level ground. His claws find traction in the dirt, but Jared leaps forward and sinks his claws into David. He howls and Jared lets go.

I peer over the edge of the hole. David has transformed back into a man. The tip of a spike pokes through his chest. His arms and legs are limp. His head hangs to the side and his eyes are still open, but the rage is gone. A sliver of moonlight shines down on glassy silver eyes.

Katie explained everything. She had been recently hired by Complimentz and didn't know how to tell me. She met David a month ago. It started off innocent with him paying for compliments from her each night. They eventually slept together, but she didn't want anything serious.

Based on what Katie told me about their fling, I'm guessing he bombed the restaurant out of anger since it was where he had met her. He told her he was using her as bait to lure me and Jared. Then he was going to force her to be his mate.

It took a while for Katie to stop having nightmares, but she's doing better now. I still have one question that hasn't been answered, though.

"What did David mean when he said you mated with me?" I ask. Jared's cheeks flare up as he plays with the hem of my dress.

"It's not what you think. We have to be with somebody in order to fully mate. I chose you, and that altered who I am, at least to another wolf. We can sense when we're attached to someone."

"Attached as in dating?" I ask.

"As in love," he replies. He runs his hand down my leg and moves closer.

"Wolves get attached very quickly," he adds with a smile. I think back to what Katie said. She was right about Jared after all. I curl my finger around the lock of hair that always falls into his face before tracing the shape of his lips.

My living room windows are open so the moonlight can stream in. Jared's skin shines and the color of his eyes has shifted to dark gold. A fiery thrill runs through my body because I understand what it means now.

Jared pulls me onto his lap and kisses me passionately. I cling onto him as he moves to my neck. I giggle when he licks me and I feel him smiling. He begins to unzip my dress, gently grazing my spine with his knuckles. His hand slides up and tugs at the roots of my hair near the nape of my neck. I gasp and arch my back. He growls softly and kisses my bare shoulder.

Jared's also answered the question I wanted to ask him the day Katie was taken. When I give my body to him, I feel desirable, beautiful, and loved. He's taught me how to unleash my natural-born freedom, and I love it.

Starlight Adventure

23

Chapter 1

Luke is already the most sought-after private detective, but, at the rate he's solving cases, he's on a rampage. I stuff the file of his latest client in our squeaky, dented cabinet before rolling back over to my desk. It's the only item in our office that's brand new. I trace the elegant silver lines that are painted on the smooth black surface. He bought it as a birthday gift for me last year, joking about how it was the only desk he could find that was smaller than me.

That's one of the reasons I like working for Luke. Despite his jokes about our size difference, he takes me seriously as an office manager. I still remember the guarded expression he wore when he interviewed me. When he asked if I had any concerns working for a werewolf, I pointed at the frame hanging above his head and repeated what it said because I truly believe in it: *If you believe in equality for all species, why are you still wary about wolves?*

He's never questioned my stance on equality since then.

As I'm double-checking my task list, Luke's voice carries over to where I'm at. His tone is polite but firm, which means he's talking to a client. Snowflakes cling to his blond hair and the collar of his jacket, rapidly melting from the heat inside the office. I sneak a peek at his butt as he rounds the corner of his desk. He plops into his seat and ends the call with an exhausted sigh.

"Even though you look like you've just been in battle, you're still handsome," I say.

Even more so than when he puts gel in his hair. Right now, it's mussed as if he's just gotten out of bed. It pairs perfectly with the light scruff on his jaw. He laughs and runs a hand through his hair.

"Not the kind of battle you're thinking of. Do you remember Paula?" he asks.

"The fairy who owns the forest resort?" I ask. That was one of our quickest cases. It turned out that a wolf had killed her chef over a stolen pair of ruby earrings.

"She convinced me to take a vacation," he said. My eyes are so wide that it feels like they're bugging out of their sockets.

"How did she convince you?" I ask. Red creeps up his neck. He tries to rub it away, but the flush ascends to his face. A nervous rush of air escapes from him.

"She figured out my secret," he replies.

"That you don't like to transform into a wolf?" I ask. Luke confided in me one night while we were working late that he prefers his human form. It's rare for a wolf to be born with blond hair. When he was young, his pack teased him while they were learning to hunt. They said he would never survive in the wild because his prey would see him coming.

I think that's the reason why he hasn't dated anyone in the past year. He's not the stereotypical dark and mysterious werewolf. He told me the last woman he was in a serious relationship with broke up with him a few days after he showed her his wolf form. It might've been a blow to his confidence. I've come to learn that, despite Luke's strong presence, he's sensitive.

"No, not that. It's actually something I've been wanting to tell you for a while. I just didn't know how to –"

My phone buzzes, alerting me to a text from my sister. I hold up my finger and ask him to pause for a second. Oh no.

She's going to be home soon. If I don't get there first, she'll try to cook dinner and end up making a mess in the kitchen. I don't want to clean up another burned fancy recipe.

"I'm so sorry, but I have to go. Can you tell me tomorrow?" I ask as I grab my purse and jacket. He smiles softly and looks down.

"Sure. Have a good night, Elena," he says. He starts sifting through some papers on his desk, but I can see his disappointment. I set my purse on my desk and sit back down in my chair.

"I can spare a few minutes," I say. Luke looks up in surprise and chuckles when I roll over to him. He always finds it amusing when I do that.

"When do you start your vacation?" I ask. He leans forward and, lately when he does that, I feel as if he sees only me.

"Tomorrow. Paula gave me two passes to the resort for the weekend."

"That's amazing! Are you taking someone or is it going to be a lone trip?" I ask. His blue eyes shine with hope.

"Well, I was hoping you'd come with me. It'd be our first date."

I imagine jumping over the desk and tackling him to the ground in delight. In reality, I gracefully and happily accept. He bursts out in the cutest smile and asks when the best time would be to pick me up tomorrow morning.

As we sort out the details, I can't help but squeal on the inside. I wasn't wrong when I sensed he was attracted to me. It's finally happening.

I bounce on my toes to quell the anticipation as I wait for Luke to pick me up. My weekend bag eagerly thumps against my side. It's overflowing with clothes, toiletries, and anything else I might need.

My sister was so happy when I told her the news. She promised that she wouldn't try any new recipes while I was gone. She ignored my protests and slipped some condoms in my bag, reminding me of her very active sex life. *"I know wolves," she said with a wink.*

An icy wind rushes by, scattering strands of hair across my face. As I tuck my hair behind my ear, my tattoo categorizing me as a human catches my eye.

I know every species – wolves, vamps, fairies, wizards, etc. – has different customs for relationships, but I've heard wolves are the most affectionate. Luke said they believe in fidelity, which is why I can't understand why they've been deemed as the inferior race. Who doesn't want someone to be faithful to them?

Snow crunches a few feet away from me, and the opening of a car door causes my heart to start thumping. Luke jogs over to me and opens his arms wide. I drop my bag and wrap my arms around him, squeezing him tight.

"You look beautiful," he says and kisses my forehead. I inhale the aroma of his body wash, envisioning a gentle breeze rustling pine trees on a bright summer day.

When he lets go, I pull him back with a playful smile. He laughs and hugs me again. From the corner of my eye, I see my sister peeking out the window. She's nodding in approval and pointing at a condom package in her hand. I wave my hand to shoo her away. I don't want Luke to think that I'm only thinking about sex.

Last night, my sister and I guessed that he waited this long to ask me out because he wanted to get to know me. His previous relationship most likely made him cautious, which is why I want him to know that I'm serious. It's more than physical for me.

Once we're in the car, he turns up the heater and turns on the radio. I lay my head on his shoulder and admire the icicles clinging onto the bare branches of the trees on the sidewalk. The morning sunlight reflects off them and, from this distance, they look like a cluster of shimmering lights.

• • • •

Paula's resort is spectacular. She's an earth fairy, which means that she can tend an area of land to her liking, even if it's opposite of the regular climate. Her brand is "Moonshine under Starlight". She doesn't serve moonshine, but the idea is to get high from nature. Become immersed in its mysteries and beauty.

An attendant leads us down a walking trail lined with rose bushes. Orange and mulberry trees are in full bloom. It's warm and some people are in bathing suits. They veer to the right where the attendant says a lake and a heated jacuzzi awaits.

She points to the large clearing on our left, explaining that is where the Starlight Show will take place tonight, if we'd like to join. Breakfast is served in each room at seven. We can choose to eat lunch and dinner with everyone or take it to our room.

When we round the corner, I gasp at the sight.

Our room is built to resemble two massive bubbles adjoined to each other. One has a bed and a fire pit encased in granite. The other has a small table, a large hammock, and a bathroom.

"If you have any questions, our staff works 24/7. We make hourly rounds on the trail or you can backtrack to reach the front office," she says. She hands Luke the keys and leaves.

"Do you want to go to the show?" he asks as we enter our room. The scent of lavender envelops me. He sets our bags on the ground and glances at the bed.

"I can sleep in the hammock," he says.

"I don't mind if we sleep in the same bed," I say. He smiles and the tips of his ears turn red. It's cute when he gets flustered, but I change the conversation so he won't think he has to make a decision now.

"I want to go to the show. When is it going to start?" I ask.

"Seven, which gives us lots of free time," he says.

"What do you want to do first?"

He closes the distance between us and picks me up. I giggle and wrap my arms around his neck. He pecks me on the lips.

"Whatever you want to do," he whispers. I slide my hands in his hair and kiss him softly.

"More of this," I say. Luke's expression melts. He kisses me deeply and slowly. My body quivers at the thought of exploring the hard lines of his muscles.

* * * *

After our make out session, Luke was in a dream state. He gazed at the scenery as we walked down the trail and nodded as I talked. I was flattered to see the effect I had on him, so I continued our walk in silence. We found a hideaway hidden behind willow vines and laid there, listening to the birds chirp until it began to grow dark.

"The show's about to start," he says. I snuggle into him and yawn.

"Let's stay here," I say. He slides his hand down to my lower back and rests his other on my hip, tightening his grip as he leans over to kiss me.

It starts off as a series of *pops!*

I ignore it and deepen the kiss. He groans when our tongues meet.

Screams echo. A rushed fluttering of wings alerts us to a flock of birds leaving the surrounding trees. Luke jerks upright. He tilts his head to the side to pinpoint the exact direction the screams are coming from.

"It's where the show is being held," he whispers. He crouches and leans forward on the balls of his feet. As he parts the vine curtain, he extends his arm toward me. I take his hand and move closer.

"It's a pack of wolves. They used guns to surprise everyone, but they've shifted now. From what I'm hearing, they kept several alive as hostages."

"What are we going to do? There's no phone reception out here," I whisper.

"I have no weapons. I didn't think to bring any. I got too relaxed," he mutters, shaking his head in anger. After a few seconds, he motions me to stand.

We slowly exit the hideaway. The walking trail is empty, but it's well lit by the lights embedded between the rose bushes. Unfortunately, the shadow it casts causes the forest to look darker than it actually is.

"We're going to find higher ground, and I'm going to call my pack," he whispers.

A wolf bursts in from the forest and clamps down on my calf. I scream as sharp, searing pain shoots up my leg. It's as if knives are ramming themselves into my muscle.

I hit the ground on my side and am dragged down the trail. Luke chases after us, but the wolf is faster. I yell for him to call his pack, hoping that I'll still be alive when he finds me.

Chapter 3

When we reach the clearing, the wolf throws me next to a dead body. I gag at what's left of her neck. It's Paula. Blood has pooled around her and darkened her red hair so that it looks black. Her necklace with the large silver leaf charm has bits of flesh on it.

Dead bodies are dispersed between people cowering and crying. I check the tattoo on a body. "W" for wizard is inked on his forearm.

The wolves purposefully killed the species who could've fended them off. The ones they kept alive must be human.

I quickly scan the area. Eight wolves guard the area. Two are in their human form. They're off to the side, talking quietly and occasionally sniffing the air. A rough, hoarse howl resounds near the clearing.

When Luke emerges, he's naked and panting. One of the men yells at the wolves. Within seconds, they've surrounded him, snarling and snapping their jaws. The same man who commanded the wolves (the alpha, I'm guessing) walks over to me and digs his heel in my injured calf. I scream but remain still, remembering what Luke taught me about the strength of wolves. Struggling will only make it worse. The man he was talking to morphs into a wolf and joins the others.

"Is this your mate?" the alpha calls out.

I've never seen Luke enraged. There's no humanity in his eyes. His upper lip curls and he slaps one of the wolves with the back of his hand. He soars across the clearing. The rest of the pack backs away, but their attention remains on him.

"I think I'll let her live and give her to one of my men," he says. Luke takes a step forward and one of the wolves attacks. The alpha keeps pressure on my leg as he watches the fight. Luke knocks the wolf unconscious after a few minutes. Blood drips down his forearm and there's a gash on his right side.

"Why didn't you shift to fight back?" the alpha asks, tilting his head in curiosity.

"Why did you attack these people like a bunch of cowards?" Luke spits. The alpha releases the pressure on my leg and moves closer to him, giving his back to the hostages. His entire pack is still focused on Luke. This is my chance.

I motion to a couple a few feet away from me to head for the forest. They shake their heads fiercely, clinging onto each other with trembling hands.

"You really don't know me?" the alpha asks. Luke remains silent. I breathe deeply to alleviate my pain as I make my way to a woman who's crying. I gently place my hand on her shoulder and point at the forest. When I mouth for her to go, she glances at the wolves and quickly scoots away.

"You can't think of any good reason why I picked this place? Or why I killed Paula?" he asks. I gasp as realization dawns on me. This is about the werewolf Luke arrested, the one who killed Paula's chef over the stolen earrings. He must've been a part of this pack, which means the alpha had Paula killed because she hired Luke to solve the case.

"You brought down one of our own!" the alpha roars. He opens his arms wide, gesturing all around.

"And for what? The work you do changes nothing! Everyone still looks down on us!"

"I take down criminals of all species. It's not my fault he chose to murder someone," Luke says.

"You're going to fix this or I'm going to kill them," he says, pointing to the hostages. The wolves break their circle around Luke and make their way toward us. Choked cries ring out. I back up to where Paula's body lies.

There has to be a weapon nearby. Something that'll catch them off guard long enough for Luke's pack to arrive. I frantically scan the area, but there's nothing. The wolves attacked when everyone was at their most vulnerable.

Out of the corner of my eye, a glint of silver flashes. A ray of moonlight shines on Paula's necklace. I swallow hard and whisper an apology to her. Then I grab the silver chain and pull.

The silver leaf is sharp and long enough to use to stab, but I need a wolf to come to me. I wipe the bits of flesh off the charm and grip it.

"Hey!" I shout. The wolf closest to me whips his head in my direction. The alpha turns around, taken aback by my outburst.

"Kill me first," I say. No one moves. Luke glances at me then looks up to the sky. The moon is full tonight and the strongest light in the clearing is where I'm at.

"Come on! Kill me. I'm right here," I say. Luke crouches down. His eyes are locked on the alpha's back. He's figured out my plan. He knows I'm buying him time.

"Do it," I yell. The alpha nods and the wolf leaps toward me.

In those seconds, Luke's voice is clear in my mind. *Everyone believes silver is a wolf's weakness, but that's not entirely true. It's silver drenched in moonlight.*

I stab the wolf in the chest as he pins me to the ground. He whimpers in agony and I throw him off me.

Luke shifts into a wolf and pounces on the alpha, biting deep into his neck. The wolves race over to help their injured leader and I shout for the hostages to run. They scramble away, disappearing into the forest.

Growling alerts me to the wolves charging in from the opposite side of the forest. Two of them yank the wolves off Luke's back. One of them finishes what Luke started and rips out a huge chunk from the alpha's neck. A wolf from the alpha's pack heads to the unconscious members.

Luke's golden white fur ripples under the moonlight with every step he takes. When the fight is over, he changes into a man and walks over to where I am.

"Your plan worked," he murmurs as he picks me up. I smile and rest my head on his sweaty, bloody shoulder.

"Best first date ever," I say. He laughs and carries me away.

"You're beautiful," I coo, petting Luke's head. His tongue hangs out of his mouth as I scratch under his chin. He rests his head on my lap and closes his eyes when I begin to knead the fur on his neck.

It took several months for my calf to heal. Luke still cringes when he looks at the scars, even though I've told him that it wasn't his fault. The attack made us realize that we can never let our guard down. If someone else tries to seek revenge, we'll be ready. He shifts into a wolf every night and checks the perimeter of my and my sister's house. When we go out on dates, I always carry pepper spray and a sharp silver object in my purse.

"I think you prefer my wolf form to my human one," Luke says. He grins and grabs his jeans off the floor.

His apartment is in a suburb next to the city. A forest borders one part of the complex, making it the perfect spot for a date night. I get our picnic basket and blanket and wait for him to finish getting dressed.

As we enter the forest, we pass by a couple sitting with their backs against a log. They're deep in conversation. They're wearing the same shirt and the saying on them matches the frame in our office about equality for all species.

"Hey, Jared!" Luke says. The man looks in our direction and a wide smile forms on his face. He raises his hand in greeting. The woman glances at my forearm. She holds up her arm and points at her tattoo to indicate she's human too. She smiles and leans into Jared.

"Jared's a wolf. He and his girlfriend, Danielle, invented the slogan," Luke says, pointing at their shirts.

"Oh, that's so cool! Thank you!" I say. They laugh and wave in response.

We head deeper into the forest and climb a steep slope. A flat bed of rock overlooks a stream bordered by dense foliage. Luke spreads out our picnic blanket on the rock. We eat all our food and talk until the sun sets. When the stars begin to appear, we lie down and gaze at the sky.

"I love you, Elena," he says as he plays with my hair.

"I love you too," I say and lean over to kiss him. I pull him on top of me and slip my hands under his shirt. He sighs as I explore his body, tracing every part that's familiar and finding new areas to make him shiver with delight. I gently bite his neck and he growls playfully.

I caress his blond hair, hoping that he never feels embarrassed about his wolf form again. I love how he stands out from the rest. I close my eyes and let him carry me into bliss.

Evening Dangers

While I'm waiting to be escorted backstage, I remember my first – and only – date with Ray. We went to my favorite local bookstore and found a cozy spot in the back. He told me about his life before he became a vampire. When he put his arm around my shoulder, I stiffened for a second. I'm sure he sensed my discomfort, but he played it off nicely.

Afterwards, I said I wasn't sure if I was ready to date. I used my new job as an editor for a small publishing company, "West Sun Press", as the excuse. He was understanding and asked if we could be friends. Despite my conflicting feelings about him being a vampire, I said yes.

Now I'm afraid I made a mistake.

Everyone in the lobby has a backstage pass to meet the cast, take pictures, and participate in a Q&A session. Ray asked me to come to the show tonight and gave me a pass. I pick at the skin around my thumb, focusing on the energetic chatter beside me.

A group of women are talking about Ray. He was a popular theater actor in London who was known for playing the courageous hero. In an interview years ago, he stated that he felt directors had typecast him, so he decided to come to America to pursue other roles. Ultimately, his plan failed because women now view him as the handsome villain with a heart of gold.

I have to tell him how I feel. If I don't, I'll think about what he might've said, and it'll gnaw at the back of my mind until I'm beyond repair.

Suddenly, the fluorescent lights overhead flicker and a wave of nausea turns all my thoughts into a gooey mess. I grip the armrest of my chair and keel over. A whisper of danger floats by. My mouth goes dry.

"Are you all right?" one of the women beside me asks. Her heavily lined eyes are staring into mine with genuine concern. The blue sequins on her dress cause color spots to burst across my vision. I blink rapidly and focus on the tattoo on her forearm.

"I will be. Thank you," I say with a small smile. She pats my shoulder and turns back to her friends.

Maybe it's because I'm growing closer to Ray, but vampires don't scare me like they used to. Growing up, I had an irrational fear of their fangs. It became worse when a boy in my third grade class dressed up as a vampire for our Halloween party. He chased me until he bit my neck. I ran out of the classroom, screaming for my parents.

I glance at the woman's tattoo again, counting the drops of blood that form a circle around the letter "V". Every magical species, including humans, is required by law to get the tattoo that classifies what they are. I'm human, but I disagree with the classification system because I have an ability the government doesn't recognize.

Ever since I was young, I've been able to sense when danger's near, though it's not always clear. Like now, for example. I can't pinpoint what or where the danger is.

I slowly sit back in my chair and take deep breaths. The water bottle I bought during intermission is wedged between my thigh and the seat. I take a few sips and swish the water in my mouth to get rid of the dryness.

"Attention, everyone! We will begin by forming a single file line," a man says. He's holding a clipboard and wearing a slim black headset. He asks for the name of the woman who's first in line and matches it to what's on his clipboard. He points to the right and gives her directions on where to find each cast member.

By the time it's my turn, the nausea is almost gone. I step forward and give him my name.

"So you're Brooke," he says with a knowing twinkle in his eyes. I smile, hoping he means it in a good way.

Ray's room is the first door on the right. When I step inside, he surprises me by picking me up and spinning me around. His smile is infectious.

"I smelled you coming," he says as the tip of his nose glides across my neck. I resist the urge to sigh and run my hand through his thick golden brown hair. When he sets me down, his hands linger on my hips. Hope blooms within me. Is he still attracted to me?

"You can stay here while I meet the rest," he says.

"I don't want to get you in trouble," I say.

"It's okay. I asked for permission."

I give in to his russet brown eyes and British accent. I sit in his lounge chair and admire his body as he greets his fans. He should've been a dancer. He's tall and has lean muscle.

Out of all the magical species, vampires are held in the highest esteem. They're considered to be the epitome of seduction and Ray is no exception. He seduced me with his kindness and humility. I wonder if that was his plan all along when he asked if we could stay friends.

Chapter 2

I didn't realize it until now, but my nausea went away as soon as I saw Ray. He knows about my abilities and he said I can talk to him about it, but I don't want to ruin the vibe of our night with something I don't fully understand.

"Chocolate chip or birthday cake?" he asks, holding out a bowl filled with cake batter balls. I close my eyes and pick one. He grabs one, throws it in the air, and swallows it whole. I laugh at the silly face he makes.

Ray invited me over to his apartment when the Q&A session was over. He had a spread of junk food and candy waiting. I wanted to eat on his balcony because it overlooks the city. I love the way the different sounds mix – cars honking, music blaring, people shouting, and cool air rushing by. And I love the lights. At the right angle, the stoplights, store lights, and skyscrapers blend together to create a dreamy, colorful panorama.

As much as I love the city at night, I wish Ray could be with me during the day. He said that was what he missed most about being human – not being able to feel the warmth of the sun on his skin. I wonder if he sees the spotlights on stage as a replacement.

"Why do you like to act?" I ask.

"Because I forget what I am. For a while, at least," he says.

"Have you always missed being human?" I ask. He finishes eating, sets his plate down, and moves closer.

"Not until I met you," he says. My body tenses in pleasure when he leans forward. He closes his eyes and inhales deeply. I reach out to slide my hands up his arms when I feel a rush of air.

My back hits a soft, firm surface. I realize we're in his bed as he moves my hair away from my neck.

"When I smelled you tonight, I knew your feelings for me had changed. I wanted to whisk you away right then and there," he says. I gasp as he gently scrapes his teeth down my neck. I can feel his fangs and I grab fistfuls of his shirt.

"Do it," I whisper. He stops and looks at me in shock.

"I want it," I say. He gets up from the bed and makes his way to the floor-to-ceiling window. The city lights cast a hazy glow over his conflicted expression.

"I found a way to be human again," he finally says.

"I didn't think that was possible," I say. He smiles sadly and walks back to sit at the edge of the bed. His voice is quiet as he caresses my leg.

"I can never be fully human, but there's a wizard who performs a spell. I'll age like a human. I won't have to drink as much blood and my abilities will diminish," he says.

"Will you be able to walk in the sunlight?" I ask.

"Yes," he replies. My heart swells at the thought of seeing Ray during the day, but I don't want him to think he has to do this. He knows about my fear of vampires, but he's helped me overcome that.

"Are you sure this is what you want?" I ask. He nods and starts kissing my leg. When he reaches my mouth, I wrap my legs around his waist and begin unbuttoning his shirt. He changes his pace to match mine.

"I want you, Brooke," he gasps, and I know he means in every way.

Ray scheduled a visit with the wizard tomorrow. He wants to celebrate when it's done. Although I'm happy for him, I can't shake the feeling there's something wrong. It swings like a pendulum in my chest before dropping to my lungs. The pendulum becomes a boulder that breaks off into splinters. I struggle to breathe. When I'm able to gulp down air, it's as if I'm inhaling poison.

"Brooke? Are you okay?" Ryder asks. He starts to rise from his seat, but I wave my hand to indicate I'm fine and force myself to smile.

"I just need some water." I reach across my desk and unscrew the bottle cap with shaky hands. Ryder shifts in his seat but remains silent. He's a good author. One of my best. His first novel was so successful that one of the big publishing companies offered him a contract, but he stayed with us.

West Sun Press specializes in novels that advocate for equality of all species. His second novel is about an interspecies romance. I was supposed to discuss the edits I made to the first three chapters with him today, but I have to end our meeting now. This feeling of danger is too strong. I have to warn Ray in case it's about his appointment with the wizard.

"Do you mind if I email you my edits tonight? I need to go home and lie down," I say.

"No, I don't mind at all. Do you need me to walk you to your car?" he asks. I start to say I'll be okay, but the room sways when I stand. My ankle caves in and I stumble forward. Ryder grabs my hand and steadies me.

"Thank you," I mumble. I hold onto him as he guides me out of my office. It's strange what I notice when I get this way. Up close, his eyes are the same shade of brown as Ray's.

• • • •

I called Ray as soon as I got home. I tried staying awake, but I slipped into a dreamless sleep as soon as I closed my eyes. Hard rapping on the front door wakes me up. Ray sighs in relief when he sees me.

"What's going on? You sounded like you were drunk in your voicemail," he says as he wraps his arms around me.

"I think you're in danger, but I don't know in what way," I say. My tongue is fuzzy and feels a bit swollen. I can't keep my eyes open. Ray picks me up and carries me to my bedroom. His voice is muffled, but I think he tells me to sleep some more.

When I wake again, it's midnight. Ray is beside me, thumbing through Ryder's novel. When he sees I'm awake, he sets the book on my nightstand.

"Hey, how are you feeling?" he asks. I've seen the book many times, but there's something about Ryder's picture that stands out to me.

"Can I see that?" I ask, pointing to the book. Ray hands it to me and waits while I study Ryder's face. His eyes are hazel in the picture. Did he get colored contacts?

"I saw something today that doesn't make sense," I say.

"Is it about Ryder?" Ray asks.

"His eyes... they were different," I say. It's possible I read my feeling wrong. Maybe Ryder's the one in danger. He doesn't know about my ability, but I can still call him to see if he's okay. I reach over Ray and grab my cell phone off my nightstand. Ryder

45

doesn't answer, so I leave him a message, using the edits to his chapters as an excuse to call me back.

Ray lies down with me and I explain to him what I saw today.

"Maybe a vampire is going to attack him and that's why you saw my eyes," he says.

"But you're one of the good ones," I say.

"I am with you," he murmurs. He pulls my shirt down to expose my shoulder and kisses my neck. When our lips meet, it's as if he's consuming my desire and giving me the hottest, rawest parts of himself.

"Hurry!" Ray shouts, pulling me forward with an ecstatic smile. I laugh as he practically leaps to the counter.

It's only been thirty minutes since the wizard performed the spell, but he says he can already feel the effects. We're at the largest indoor mini golf in the city for our celebration. The entire facility glows in the dark. One round includes 36 holes and the theme is pirates. Ray pays for our round and the attendant shows us where to find our golf clubs and balls.

Ryder called me earlier today and said he could discuss the edits tomorrow. He sounded normal and asked how I was doing. I was relieved to know he was okay, but it brought me back to my original question: What is the danger I've been feeling?

Ray pulls me out of my worry when I see that he can't stop smiling. When we enter the play area, a wax statue of a menacing pirate greets us. He's dressed entirely in red and tells us in an exaggerated accent to beware of the changing sea.

Surprisingly, we're the only ones in the first section. It contains 18 holes and a black curtain conceals the second section. Fish, coral reefs, and hammerhead sharks are painted on the black walls in neon colors. Sea-themed obstacles creatively block the path to each hole.

After the third hole, I start to think that the spell needs more time to take effect. Ray is consistently making holes-in-one while I struggle to get my ball in the hole. Granted, I've never been great at mini golf, but his swings are too smooth. When I tell Ray about my suspicion, he laughs.

"My abilities diminished, but they didn't completely go away," he says as places his hand on my waist.

"I can teach you," he whispers in my ear. His hot breath sends a jolt of passion through my body. The thought of having sex while a gigantic fish stares at me causes me to giggle uncontrollably. Ray laughs at my reaction and kisses me.

We're at the last hole of the first section when an invisible knife jabs me in the back. All the air is pushed out of my lungs. I gasp frantically. Now I know.

The danger is tonight and we need to get out of here.

I can't see past the black curtain that divides the sections, but I'm guessing each exit is the same distance from where we're at. The lights shut off as I turn to Ray. He grabs my hand, but it doesn't stop me from screaming. We're in pitch-black darkness.

An electric whirring sounds. The lights come back on, flickering rapidly. Color spots fill my vision. I yell for Ray to get us out of here. He scoops me up and rushes past the black curtain.

Something knocks into him from behind and we fall to the ground. A figure zooms by me, picks up Ray, and throws him against the wall. There's only one species fast enough to do that.

"Vampire," I whisper.

I slowly stand, looking both ways. I cup my hand over my mouth to keep from screaming when I notice bodies with their necks twisted at unnatural angles. I gag at the sight of their protruding bones. Ray is slowly rising and wincing in pain. Before I can take another step, he's slammed into the wall again and falls to the ground. This time, he doesn't move. I run over to him and put his arm around my shoulders, even though I know we won't make it out of here if the vampire wants to kill us. My legs are shaking and Ray is too heavy for me.

"Hello, Brooke," a familiar voice says. Ryder places a cloth over my mouth and nose, filling me with a chemical scent. I claw at his hands and wrists, but the poison is too strong. My mind grows foggy and my limbs become heavy. The last thing I see is Ray lying on the floor unconscious.

In that moment, he looks completely human.

Chapter 5

Something soft and cold trails down my leg. I turn to my side and swat it away. Memories tug at the back of my mind. They're faint and wispy, as if I'm grasping at smoke.

"Wake up, Brooke," a voice whispers. Whatever was on my leg moves to my arm. The image of Ray asleep flashes in my mind, but I don't understand why I need to remember that.

"Time to wake up."

I know that voice. Ryder might be able to tell me what's going on. I try to speak, but my mouth is dry. When I open my eyes, Ray brings a cup to my lips. Water slides down my throat, calming the itchiness.

My vision clears, but it takes me a few seconds to realize it's not Ray. It's Ryder with brown eyes and hair dyed the exact same shade as Ray's. He's even wearing the clothes Ray had on tonight.

I can't control my breathing as the events that happened earlier tonight crash into me. Ryder has become a vampire. He killed people and attacked us.

"Why?" I ask. He strokes my neck with the tip of his finger.

"I thought I had more time. I underestimated his ability to seduce. It's obvious you don't want a human man, so I decided to become like him. I'm hoping it'll make it easier for you to fall in love with me," he says. A tear slides down my cheek and my voice cracks when I speak.

"Did you kill him?" I ask.

"Not yet," he replies. He helps me into a sitting position. We're in a living room filled with antique furniture. Across from us is a lighted fireplace. A grandfather clock stands in one corner.

Its large golden pendulum swings back and forth as the minute hand moves closer to midnight.

Everything I was sensing the past few days is clear now. The lights, the nausea, the sleepiness, the poison, the pendulum. It was leading up to this moment.

This can't be real. I know Ryder. He's not crazy.

"You're not a killer," I say.

"You're right. I wasn't planning on killing. I gave Ray the idea to become human. Actually, no. That's not true. I gave the idea to someone who knew him, but I wasn't expecting you to stay with him. I had to come up with Plan B, so... here we are," he says.

He walks over to the fireplace and picks up the poker that's propped against the brick wall. He tosses it between his hands and heads back to the couch. I cringe when he sets it down beside him. Ryder sees my reaction and grabs my shoulders.

"I would never hurt you, Brooke," he says. The pressure he's applying isn't enough to hurt me and his expression is serious.

"I believe you," I say, though I know he won't hesitate to kill Ray. He lets me go and resumes his original position. Ray is probably already tracking me, and Ryder's waiting for him. I have to tread carefully.

"Why didn't you tell me how you felt earlier?" I ask.

"I had to make sure you were the one, but Ray swooped in while I was doing that. I admire his determination to have you, but your relationship needs to end. You belong to me," he says, reaching out to caress my hair. I consider going for the poker now, but it's closer to him. He'd snatch it before I could reach for it.

Ryder perks up and glances behind me.

"Showtime," he whispers, narrowing his eyes at the front door. Ryder stands with the poker in his hand. The door creaks open, but the porch is empty.

"You're not as fast as me anymore," he shouts. The silence that follows rings in my ears. A floorboard groans when Ryder takes a step forward. The stench of gasoline fills the room as Ryder is doused in gas.

A red canister hits him in the face. Ray appears in front of him and shoves him toward the fireplace. He tries to grab the poker, but Ryder hangs on tight. He sends Ray across the room, but Ray is ready. He lands on his feet. They collide into each other and the poker clatters to the floor.

Ryder gets on top of Ray and starts punching him in the face. Ray punches him in the stomach, but it's not enough to get Ryder off him. Ryder is drawing blood with each jab.

I need to set Ryder on fire. I search for anything flammable and spot the fireplace lighter on the coffee table. It takes me a few tries, but I produce a small flame. I don't know if Ryder will sense me coming or if he's completely focused on Ray, so I tiptoe toward him. When I'm close enough, I jab his bicep. He screams as fire erupts on his body.

Ray's shirt is stained with gasoline. I sink my nails in his shoulders and drag him away. Ryder runs toward us, but Ray kicks his shin. He falls to the ground as Ray rises.

"You can never be me," Ray says. Then he kicks him in the face. Ryder completely drops to the ground as his body is devoured by the flames.

Being with Ray during the day is everything I thought it would be. He cherishes the warmth of the summer season and loves it when he sweats. He leaves his balcony door open and lets the hot air blow in.

The nightmares come and go, but Ray is always there to calm me. I don't ignore my ability anymore. Whenever I sense danger, I analyze it. Ray listens when I need to talk about it, and we do our best to figure it out together.

We're finishing up our ice cream as we head to a nearby jewelry market. The clouds are large and puffy and the sunrays are visible today. I point it out to Ray and he stops to take a good look.

"Amazing," he breathes.

"Do you think you'll ever miss having the full strength of a vampire?" I ask. He turns to me with a look in his eyes I haven't seen until now. He's at peace.

"Not if it means I have to lose out on this," he says. His smile lights up his face, and it's as if sunlight itself lives within him.

"This is my happily ever after," he says. He kisses me and he tastes like vanilla and strawberry. It's the perfect combination on a serene summer day.

Midnight Perils

54

Modern gypsies don't tell fortunes for a living. We aren't nomadic. From time to time, we see the future, but we don't need a crystal ball. We don't steal or lie. I'm personally offended by this stereotype. We're not the only race that's ever stolen or told a lie.

Modern gypsies love fashion. We accessorize our outfits with jewelry. Lots of jewelry. I own a small jewelry market and everything I sell is designed by me. Depending on the season, I set up my stand in the city's plaza or the mall. I've steadily built my customer base, but tourists come during the summer, which makes it my busiest season.

The banner displaying my business name, "Gypsy Jewel", billows in the hot breeze. I glance at my sister's bakery across the street, wishing I had bought two cups of lemon-flavored ice. Right now, I'm bombarded with customers. Normally, that would excite me, but I've been sweating since this morning. My underarms are drenched and, although I've put my hair in a ponytail, sweat continues to pour down the nape of my neck.

My next customers are a couple. She's buying a lot of jewelry, and her boyfriend is smiling at her dreamily. It's rare to see a vampire during the day. He looks so calm, despite the sweltering heat. I recognize him from the posters around the plaza that are advertising a theater play.

"I know you! You're Ray, right?" I ask. He blinks as if he's waking up.

"That's right. I'm that guy," he says, pointing to his character on the poster that's stapled to the nearest tree. He takes out his credit card and hands it to me. When I touch it, I see them getting married on the beach. She's in a sundress and wearing one of my necklaces. I charge them for everything but that necklace. She hesitates to take it when I tell her it's free.

"Are you sure?" she asks.

"A gift for a special occasion," I say. She glances at Ray, who's holding an earring to the sunlight and gazing at the dangling gems. I smile and discreetly point at my ring finger. Her eyes widen and she takes the necklace.

The rest of the day passes by quickly. After my sister helps me pack up my jewelry, we eat ice cream cake for dinner.

"Have you heard about the latest killing?" Ellie asks. She knows I never keep up with the news, so her asking is a segue into what she's going to tell me. I scrape the last bit of frosting off the top of my cake slice and wait.

"He's growing bolder. A body was found in the alley behind Complimentz, the restaurant that was bombed a year ago," she says.

"How do you know it's a he?" I ask. She glances around as if someone might hear her, even though we're safely locked in her restaurant. I take the opportunity to finish her cake slice.

"Just a feeling. The police have officially labeled him a serial killer, so we need to be careful," she says.

"He targets werewolves, remember?" I say. She gives me a look that says I'm being too nonchalant about this. I apologize and show her the mace I always carry in my purse.

"I'll be careful," I say. She smiles with satisfaction before looking down at her empty plate. I laugh at her shocked expression and get up to grab the rest of the cake off the counter.

When we leave, it's close to ten. Our apartment is a block away. We usually cut through the plaza because the streetlamps give off a bright white light.

Each summer, our city hosts a world-renowned festival celebrating nature. My jewelry contains natural crystals, and because my business is well-known, I've been given a permanent spot in the festival by the city government. I can't distinguish my empty stand from the others right now, but I know it's there with my banner folded neatly on top of the table. Despite it being hot and busy today, I'm excited to do it again tomorrow.

I slow my pace when I spot a group of fireflies hanging around a birch tree. They look like tiny orbs of golden light from this distance. One of them breaks from the group.

"Hey there," I say as it flitters around me. I try to cup it in my hands, but it dodges me. It leads me to a large tree planted at the edge of the plaza.

"Lana! You scared me. I turned around and you weren't there," Ellie says. She places her hands on her hips, panting.

I don't answer because I'm stunned by the dark liquid at the base of the trunk. The grass is stained with it as well, and there's more on the other side. I walk around and come face-to-face with a gruesome sight.

Ellie screams at the wolf that's lying on the ground, bleeding profusely. When I bend down, she grabs my hand.

"What are you doing? Let's go! The killer could still be here," she shrieks.

"We don't know what happened to him. He needs help. Can you get our car and park at the curb?" I ask. She looks at me in disbelief.

"Or we could call the police," she says.

"They were forced to address the murders. And even if he made it to the ER, do you really think he would get the proper care?" I ask.

Ellie protests when I take a closer look at him. His breathing is ragged and his wounds are deep. Whoever did this had claws.

When it's clear that Ellie's not taking me seriously, I gesture for her to get moving. She groans and stomps in the direction of our apartment.

While I wait for her, I stroke a patch of the wolf's fur that isn't matted with blood. If this was the serial killer's work, he made a mistake by not making sure he finished the job.

Chapter 2

One month later

"He's become attached to you," Ellie says with a small smile. My wolf is beside me, watching as I flip his steaks in the frying pan. I pet his head and he rubs against my side. I laugh when he licks his lips. He knows the food is for him.

After Ellie and I got him inside our apartment, I called our mom. She had taught us how to take care of wounds when we were kids, but I wasn't sure if I remembered correctly, so she guided Ellie and I through the process.

He was unconscious the entire time. After we stitched him up, we carried him to my bed where he stayed for two weeks. When he was able to walk, he began following me everywhere, even to work.

All magical species (wolves, vamps, fairies, wizards, etc.) publicly coexist with humans. For some strange – and stupid – reason, werewolves are known as the inferior race. Of course, not everyone dislikes wolves, but I noticed that some people backed away from my stand when they saw him beside me. He whined when he noticed it, as if he was apologizing to me, but I told him not to worry about it. The only customers I want are the ones who believe in equality for all species.

So far, he hasn't shifted into a human yet. Ellie theorized that staying in his wolf form would speed up the healing process. I've put flyers around the city with a picture of his wolf face in case anyone's reported him missing, but no one has come for him.

"Do you have any family?" I ask as I place the steaks on his plate. He grunts in response and rips into the meat.

"Like he's really going to answer with a 'yes' or 'no,'" Ellie says with a snort. I ignore her and run my hand through his black fur.

Ellie's not against wolves. She's just scared the serial killer is going to come back to finish the job. She hasn't said it aloud, but I know she's anxious for him to leave.

"I'm going to take a shower. I'll let you know when you can come to the room," I tell him.

"Be nice," I mouth to Ellie. She makes a face and heads to her room.

After my shower, I find him resting on his back with his legs in the air. I laugh and scratch his belly to wake him up. He runs to my room and jumps on top of my bed.

"You must be completely healed if you're able to do that," I say. He trots all over my mattress until he finds a good spot. When I lay down, he rests his head on top of my stomach.

"Do you prefer your wolf form?" I ask. He blinks but remains quiet.

"It's okay if you do. I think wolves are beautiful," I say. He huffs and licks my hand. I stroke his head and talk to him about whatever comes to my mind.

"You know you can go home whenever you want to. I really thought someone would've come for you by now. Are you from out of town?" I ask. He whines and nuzzles my hand. Judging from his reaction, his pack must be a delicate subject. I switch to a lighter topic and pet him until we fall asleep.

· · · ·

Shimmery rays of sunlight filter through my window blinds. I roll over, determined to stay in this halfway state between dreams and reality. My sheets are warm, but my pillow is cold.

The scent of lavender and fresh dirt surrounds me. I don't know if birds are chirping outside my window or if it's my imagination.

Something soft and hot touches my neck and travels down to my shoulder. When I sigh in pleasure, the sensation stops. I roll onto my back and soak in the sunlight through my closed eyelids.

As I'm falling back asleep, I feel something touch my lips. I jerk awake to a man on top of me. I scream and kick him in the groin. He grunts in pain and falls over. I jump out of bed and land on a pile of fresh flower petals. They're scattered around my room. A bouquet of carnations is on top of my desk along with a tray of breakfast food.

"Lana, wait! It's me," the man says. His hands are raised slightly, as if to show he means no harm. He's tall and built with wavy black hair and dark blue eyes. My wolf's eyes. He's dressed, but his feet are bare and smeared with dirt. My breathing slows down as I realize he must've done this while I was asleep.

"I didn't mean to scare you. I wanted to surprise you," he says, lowering his hands.

"What's your name?" I ask.

"Trent," he replies.

"Why haven't you shifted into a human before?"

"Your sister was right. I remained a wolf so I could heal faster. When I became strong enough, I wanted to change, but I was nervous. I saw how comfortable you were with me as a wolf. I wasn't sure if you would act the same when I changed into a man," he says.

I study him for a few minutes. He shifts in his stance and clears his throat, clearly uncomfortable with my silent observation. I've heard wolves can get attached quickly.

Romance didn't cross my mind when Ellie mentioned it last night, but I see it now.

Trent has feelings for me. My heart beats wildly when I remember him on top of me. Can I see him in that way? I've only known his wolf side.

"Thank you for this," I say, gesturing to the flowers and food. He smiles, but there's sadness in his eyes. He must sense that I'm cautious.

"Let's eat in here," I say. He perks up a bit and grabs the tray off my desk. My stomach rumbles when I see a blueberry bagel smothered in cream cheese.

"My favorite," I say. He smiles and sits so that our shoulders are touching. We eat in silence for a few minutes, but I'm curious to find out.

"What happened the night I found you? Did someone attack you?" I ask. He gestures to the door with his bagel in hand.

"Your sister was right again," he says as the door opens. Ellie's mouth drops when she sees Trent. I motion for her to come in, but she remains in the doorway, stunned.

"Good morning to you too, big sis," I say as Trent waves at her. She turns around in a daze and walks away.

"What just happened?" he asks. I laugh and reach for a granola bar.

"She likes you," I say.

Trent was attacked by the serial killer the night we found him. He changed into a wolf, thinking that would give him an advantage, but it didn't. The killer ripped into him with his claws and teeth. When Trent was sure the killer was gone, he dragged himself to the park, hoping someone would find him, and passed out.

Ellie gasped in all the right places and shuddered when Trent described the killer as "faceless". But that wasn't the biggest shock.

Trent has been tracking the killer. His entire pack was slaughtered a little over a year ago. Trent survived because he was called in to work at the last minute. When he arrived at the scene, he was able to pick up the killer's scent before the police took over. They eventually declared it a random attack at the time, stating that there wasn't enough evidence to look further into it.

"He knows how to cover his tracks. I can't get ahold of his scent long enough to pinpoint him. I'm not even sure if he knew I was onto him before he attacked me," Trent finishes.

"Why do you think he's only targeting werewolves?" I ask.

"Isn't it obvious? It goes back to his pack," Ellie says. When Trent and I stare at her, she continues.

"Your entire pack was killed. He's only killing one wolf at a time now, and who do they all resemble?" Ellie asks, pointing to Trent.

"You should've been a cop," I say. She smiles and shrugs.

"But there's no one I can think of that would be an enemy," he says.

"Were you able to identify what species he was? That could be a good starting point," I say.

"His scent is unlike anything I've ever smelled before," he replies. All of us fall into a thoughtful silence.

At first, I think we have the advantage if the killer believes Trent's dead, but I dismiss that thought when I remember the media. Excluding Trent's pack, they've broadcasted every kill. It's possible the killer waited for them to report Trent's death. I also taped flyers around the city. He might've seen one and realized Trent's alive.

"He's going to come back to finish the job," Ellie says.

"Then why hasn't he?" I ask.

"He probably knows you are gypsies," Trent says.

"The killer is afraid of gypsies?" Ellie asks. I bite my lip, resisting the urge to laugh at her skepticism.

"You're the only ones who can see the future clearly. Maybe he's afraid you'll see who he is," Trent says.

"It doesn't work that way. We can't choose what we see. Sometimes, we go months without seeing anything," I say.

"But maybe he doesn't know that," Trent points out. Ellie rises from her seat and claps her hands in conclusion.

"Then there's only one way to end this," she says and heads to her room. When she comes back, she's holding an orange flyer. With a flourish, she reveals what's written on it. A carnival is opening tomorrow and will run for one week.

"You have to make a public appearance," she says.

"It's going to be crowded. I don't think he'll try to finish the job there," I say.

"But it could anger him. He might think that Trent is flaunting his survival. And... it's a cute first date," she says, waggling her eyebrows at us. Trent blushes. I smile at my sister's idea. She's managed to set a trap to expose the killer and plan a date for Trent and me at the same time.

"Why aren't you more excited? Trent is gorgeous," Ellie says, falling onto her bed dramatically. I'm searching through her closet for the finishing touches for my outfit. Underneath a pile of shirts, I find her pink hip scarf with the dangling silver coins and the matching earrings.

"We could be going to our deaths," I say. She waves her hand at me, dismissing my response.

"I know that you're not," she sings.

"Did you have a vision?" I ask as I wrap the scarf around my hips. She nods excitedly and gets up to close her bedroom door.

"I didn't see the details, so don't gross out. All I know is: You. Trent. Best sex of your life."

I burst out laughing at her summary. She joins in and we stay in that bubble of contentment until reality sets in. We have a killer to catch.

• • • •

I haven't been to a carnival since I was a kid. I forgot how much I like the atmosphere. The scent of buttery popcorn and cotton candy fills the air. Crushed popcorn kernels and corn dog wrappers litter the ground. Children weave in between people, chasing each other with flashing wands or swords. Vendors sell knick-knacks, snow globes, and glow bracelets at almost every corner. Stuffed animals hang from the ceiling or are piled on shelves at every game stand.

Trent picks one of my favorite games to play. It's a racing game that requires every player to shoot water into a tiny hole with a water nozzle. How much water they're able to get in the hole determines how fast or slow their plastic seahorse moves toward the finish line.

I give it my best, but Trent wins in the end. The game attendant flinches when Trent reaches for the prize and quickly hands it over. Trent's tattoo identifying him as a werewolf is on full display tonight.

By law, every species is required to get a tattoo to identify what they are. I've added more detail to mine. The sun that encloses the letter "H" for human is bigger and one of the rays dips into a crescent moon. Interspecies romances are not rare, but they're not common either. The game attendant sneers at me when she glances at my forearm. I ignore her reaction and happily accept the stuffed elephant from Trent.

Ellie calls to check up on us, but there's nothing to report. She's doing fine at home. I know I don't have to worry about her. She has an array of weapons that targets each species' weaknesses. If the killer comes after her, he doesn't stand a chance.

"I like this," Trent says as he plays with the silver coins that are attached to my hip scarf. I wiggle my hip a bit and he laughs as they clink against each other.

"Do you make jewelry for men?" he asks.

"I've never thought about that. What would you like me to make?" I ask. He slides his hand in mine and thinks about it for a minute.

"Anything with a wolf pawprint on it," he says. I stop and motion for him to bend down. When he does, I give him a quick kiss on the lips.

"Done," I whisper. He smiles and kisses me again. I decide that I definitely like human Trent better than wolf Trent.

We play some more games until my arms are loaded with stuffed animals. When we start getting hungry, we make our way to the center of the carnival where food stands surround picnic tables. I claim an empty table by dumping all my prizes on it while Trent goes to buy us corn dogs.

I hear the ear-piercing breaking of metal before I see the Ferris wheel crashing. The ground shakes. An uproar arises. People are running and screaming. Children are shouting for their parents. I can't find Trent in the crowd. I'm making my way to the parking lot when I notice a man dressed in black by the Ferris wheel.

His back is facing me. He's kneeling and his head is bobbing, as if he's eating. Blood is splattered on the ground and on the metal rods of the Ferris wheel. An arm is on the ground beside the man. I gasp when I realize it's detached from a body. The man jerks upright and spins around. Now I know why Trent described the killer as faceless. He's wearing a black mask with a slit for his mouth.

I scream for Trent, hoping he hears me above the roar of the crowd. When I turn to hightail it to the parking lot, I bump into him.

He throws me over his shoulder and runs. By the time we make it to the parking lot, it's deserted. When we're inside the car, the killer jumps on top of the hood. Trent shouts for me to hold on tight and puts the car into drive. He heads for a nearby tree, but the killer realizes Trent's intention and jumps off. Trent turns the wheel and the back of the car bumps into the tree trunk.

As I'm taking out the pocketknife Ellie gave me for protection, my car door is ripped open and I soar across the parking lot. Trent shouts for me, but I can't speak. My stomach is in my throat until I land on my side on the gravel. Before my body can react to the pain, the killer has his hands around my throat.

Suddenly, he cries out in pain and falls to the ground. When my vision clears, I see Trent holding my pocketknife. It's dripping with blood. Ellie didn't know what we might come up against, but she gave me a knife made entirely of silver in case the killer was a werewolf.

Trent rips off the killer's mask. Under the light of the full moon, his face constantly shifts between a wolf and a man. All of his teeth are as sharp as vampire fangs. Blood spurts out of his mouth. I scramble away from him and stand behind Trent while he stares at the killer in disbelief.

"Jeremy?" he says. Jeremy coughs and winces in pain.

"Surprised?" he asks.

"What happened to you?" Trent asks. Jeremy wipes some blood away from the corners of his mouth.

"The spell went bad. Instead of becoming a vampire, I ended up like this. I killed Michelle by accident," he says. Trent kneels down and brushes away some hair from Jeremy's forehead.

"Why did you kill our pack? Dad would've taken you back," he says. Jeremy chuckles.

"I did come back. Dad rejected me. He said the entire pack would too. I hadn't had blood in a while. I lost it in that moment," he says.

"Why didn't you come to me?"

Jeremy's breathing grows raspy. He struggles to clear his throat. Trent lifts his head so he can speak.

"I was so angry and jealous. You were always the favorite. When I realized you were still alive, I couldn't bring myself to kill you. On the night I attacked you, I didn't even know it was you. I was so thirsty for blood. Sometimes, all I can think about is killing and eating. When I realized it was you, I was conflicted. I stayed away until I couldn't. When I saw you had found a new family, I snapped."

Jeremy coughs up more blood. Trent gently lays his head on the ground. A tear falls out of his eye and lands on Jeremy's cheek. Jeremy smiles weakly and closes his eyes.

"Thank you," he sighs.

"For what?" Trent asks.

"For taking away the pain," he says.

Jeremy was Trent's older brother. When they were in high school, he left the pack to live with his girlfriend, Michelle, who was a vampire. Jeremy wanted to become a vampire for Michelle, even though he knew that certain species, such as werewolves, can't become vampires. He went to a wizard for help, but the spell the wizard did ended up turning him into a hybrid. It's why Trent wasn't able to identify his scent.

Trent assumed that Jeremy killed werewolves out of jealousy, wishing he could have what he lost. I don't think Jeremy consciously knew he was killing wolves who looked like Trent.

It took some time for Trent to mourn. I stayed up with him on his sleepless nights. Some days, he would remain in his wolf form, following me everywhere. Eventually, he rose out of his sadness.

Ellie serves us another plate of strawberry jam cookies with sprinkles. Trent eats half of the plate and tries to steal my side as well. I laugh at his playfulness, remembering how I did that to Ellie on the night I found him. When he's not looking, she gives me a thumbs-up, signaling that tonight's the night. Her vision is coming true.

After we finish eating, Trent and I head to the beach. It's an hour away from the city. By the time we arrive, everyone is gone. The waves are crashing onto the shore. Saltwater sprays my feet and the wind ruffles my hair. Trent spreads out our beach towel near the pier.

I rest my back against his chest and he wraps his arms around me. I listen to the smooth timbre of his voice, drifting to sleep until I remember what I have for him. His face lights up when I take out a silver necklace. He studies the medium-sized pendant.

A wolf pawprint is engraved on it and so is Jeremy's name.

"It's beautiful," he says.

After he puts it on, he kisses me. It's a sweet kiss that becomes something deeper. It's passionate and full of love but something more. I can't figure out what it is until his hands begin exploring my body. Trent is ravishing me. He opens his mouth wide when he kisses me, as if he's consuming me.

"Can I make you my mate?" he whispers.

I lean forward and gently bite his bottom lip and he gasps. I giggle at his stunned reaction.

"Yes," I say. When he smiles, I'm propelled into our future.

Trent's sitting down, playing with a baby who has a tuft of black hair. I stand in the doorway, watching as he bounces him up and down. The baby laughs and touches Trent's face with his tiny hand.

When I come back to the present, Trent's lips are burning. His shirt is off and I'm running my hands down the curve of his back. A part of me is nervous about what comes next, but I find comfort in Trent's touches and cherish our future together.

❖ Follow – Martin Garrix & Zedd
o For the entire series
❖ I'm Good (Blue) – David Guetta & Bebe Rexha
(Clean Version)
o For *Moonlight Thrills*
❖ Feel So Right – Krystal Meyers
o For *Starlight Adventure*
❖ Supermassive Black Hole – Muse
o For *Evening Dangers*
❖ Hanging By A Moment – Lifehouse
o For *Midnight Perils*

Also by Genevieve Leanne Dominguez

The Moonlight Thrills Series
Moonlight Thrills
Starlight Adventure
Evening Dangers
Midnight Perils
The Moonlight Thrills Series: The Complete Collection

Standalone
When I Dream of You
Phoenix: A Small Poetry Collection

Watch for more at https://genevieveleanne.wixsite.com/mysite.

About the Author

Genevieve Leanne Dominguez, born and raised in Texas, now lives on the East Coast. She earned a B.A. in English from the University of Central Florida in 2020.

Writing, editing, and self-publishing her books is her primary hobby. Her goal is to entertain readers or help readers learn something positive. She would love to do that for many readers, but if she could do that for just one reader, then she will have done what she has set out to do as an indie author.

She likes playing video games and finding new music. She loves the autumn season and her favorite days are cloudy, rainy days. Werewolves and phoenixes are her favorite mythical creatures.

Visit her website to contact her.

Read more at https://genevieveleanne.wixsite.com/mysite.